W9-CKH-902

I'm going to read

UP TO
100
WORDS

I'm Going To **READ!**™

These levels are meant only as guides;
you and your child can best choose a book that's right.

Level 1: Kindergarten–Grade 1 . . . Ages 4–6
- word bank to highlight new words
- consistent placement of text to promote readability
- easy words and phrases
- simple sentences build to make simple stories
- art and design help new readers decode text

Level 2: Grade 1 . . . Ages 6–7
- word bank to highlight new words
- rhyming texts introduced
- more difficult words, but vocabulary is still limited
- longer sentences and longer stories
- designed for easy readability

Level 3: Grade 2 . . . Ages 7–8
- richer vocabulary of up to 200 different words
- varied sentence structure
- high-interest stories with longer plots
- designed to promote independent reading

Level 4: Grades 3 and up . . . Ages 8 and up
- richer vocabulary of more than 300 different words
- short chapters, multiple stories, or poems
- more complex plots for the newly independent reader
- emphasis on reading for meaning

Note to Parents

What a great sense of achievement it is when you can accomplish
a goal! With the **I'm Going To Read!**™ series, goals are established
when you pick up a book. This series was developed to grow with
the new reader. The vocabulary grows quantifiably from 50 different
words at Level One, to 100 different words at Level Two, to 200 different
words at Level Three, and to 300 different words at Level Four.

Ways to Use the Word Bank

- Read along with your child and help him or her sound out
  the words in the word bank.

- Have your child find the word in the word bank as you
  read it aloud.

- Ask your child to find the word in the word bank that
  matches a picture on the page.

- Review the words in the word bank and then ask your child
  to read the story to you.

Related Word Bank Activities

- Create mini-flash cards in your handwriting. This provides
  yet another opportunity for the reader to be able to identify
  words, regardless of what the typography looks like.

- Think of a sentence and then place the mini-flash cards
  on a table out of order. Ask your child to rearrange the
  mini-flash cards until the sentence makes sense.

- Make up riddles about words in the story and have your
  child find the appropriate mini-flash card. For example,
  "It's red and it bounces. What is it?"

- Choose one of the mini-flash cards and ask your child
  to find the same word in the text of the story.

- Create a second set of mini-flash cards and play a game
  of Concentration, trying to match the pairs of words.

LEVEL 2

2   4   6   8   10   9   7   5   3   1

Published by Sterling Publishing Co., Inc.
387 Park Avenue South, New York, NY 10016
Text © 2008 by Harriet Ziefert, Inc.
Illustrations © 2008 by Mark Chambers
Distributed in Canada by Sterling Publishing
c/o Canadian Manda Group, 165 Dufferin Street,
Toronto, Ontario, Canada M6K 3H6
Distributed in the United Kingdom by GMC Distribution Services,
Castle Place, 166 High Street, Lewes, East Sussex, England BN7 1XU
Distributed in Australia by Capricorn Link (Australia) Pty. Ltd.
P.O. Box 704, Windsor, NSW 2756, Australia

I'm Going To Read is a trademark of Sterling Publishing Co., Inc.

Library of Congress Cataloging-in-Publication Data

Chambers, Mark, 1980–
  Pass the food, dude / pictures by Mark Chambers.
    p. cm.—(I'm going to read)
  "Text copyright 2008 by Harriet Ziefert, Inc."
  ISBN-13: 978-1-4027-5545-3
  ISBN-10: 1-4027-5545-7
  [1. Dinners and dining—Fiction.] I. Harriet Ziefert, Inc. II. Title.

PZ7.C3566Pas 2008
[E]—dc22   2007029924

Sterling ISBN-13: 978-1-4027-5545-3
ISBN-10: 1-4027-5545-7

For information about custom editions, special sales, and premium
and corporate purchases, please contact Sterling Special Sales Department
at 800-805-5489 or specialsales@sterlingpub.com.

PASS THE FOOD, DUDE!

STERLING
New York / London
www.sterlingpublishing.com/kids

Pass the food, dude!

egg bread

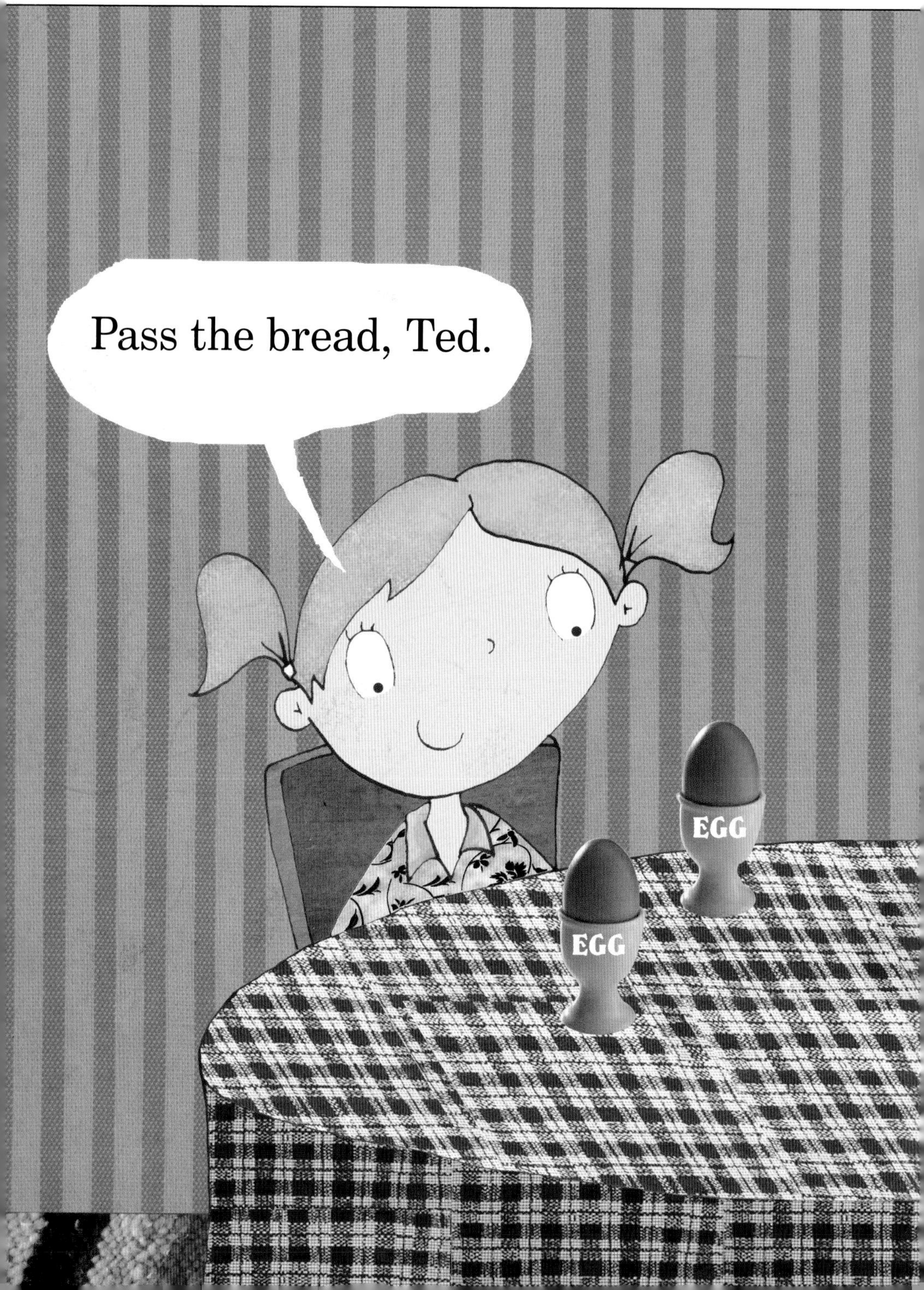

Pass the cheese,
Louise.

Pass the meat,
Pete.

Pass the frank,
Hank.

Pass the ham,
Sam.

Pass the juice, Bruce.

Pass the soda, Rhoda.

Pass the sushi, Lucy.

Pass the soy, Joy.

Pass
the wasabi,
Bobby.

Pass
the tea,
Lee.

Pass the chili, Lily.

Pass the fajita, Rita.

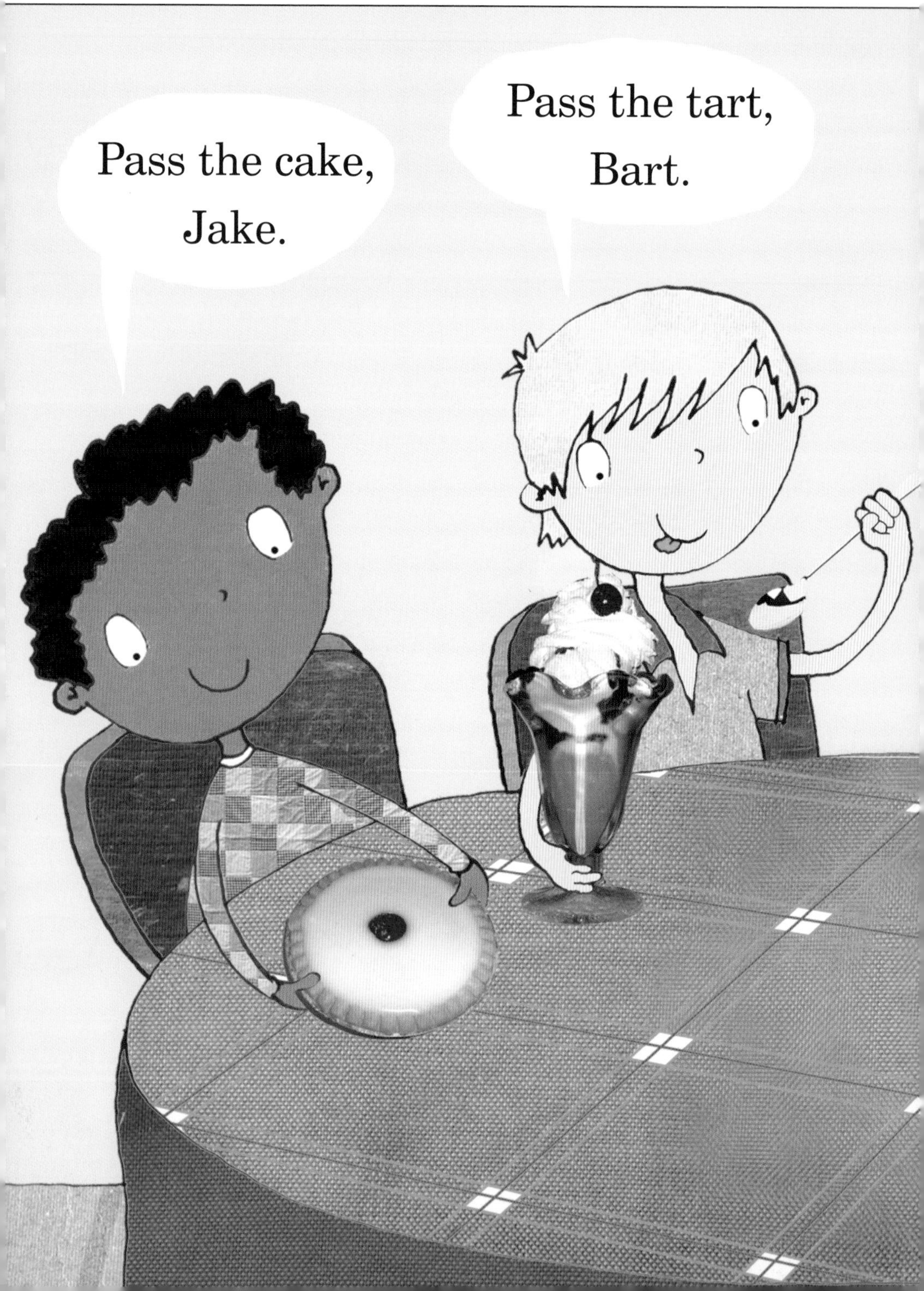
Pass the cake,
Jake.
Pass the tart,
Bart.

Pass the papaya,
Maya.

Pass the banana,
Anna.

Pass the cherry, Kerry.

Pass the plates, mates!

JUV
EASY
Ziefert

Ziefert, Harriet.

Pass the food, dude!

DUE DATE   3.95
